AMULET OF AVANTIA

→ BOOK TWENTY-FOUR ←

STEALTH
THE GHOST PANTHER

JAN   2014

BEASTQUEST®

AMULET OF AVANTIA

⤙ BOOK TWENTY-FOUR ⤚

STEALTH
THE GHOST PANTHER

ADAM BLADE

ILLUSTRATED BY EZRA TUCKER

SCHOLASTIC INC.

With special thanks to Cherith Baldry

For Adam Dawkins

ISBN 978-0-545-27215-5

Beast Quest series created by Beast Quest Ltd., London.
BEAST QUEST is a trademark of Beast Quest Ltd.

Text © 2009 by Beast Quest Ltd. All rights reserved.
Cover illustration © 2009 by Steve Sims
Interior illustrations © 2012 by Scholastic Inc.

Published by Scholastic Inc., 557 Broadway, New York, NY 10012, by arrangement with Working Partners Ltd.
SCHOLASTIC and associated logos are trademarks and/or registered trademarks of Scholastic Inc.

12 11 10 9 8 7 6 5 4 3 2 1   12 13 14 15 16 17/0

Designed by Tim Hall
Printed in the U.S.A.   40
First printing, September 2012

BEAST QUEST

AMULET OF AVANTIA

BEASTQUEST

CHARACTER GUIDE

HEROES AND VILLAINS

⤙ TOM ⤚

PREFERRED WEAPONS: Sword and magic shield

ALSO CARRIES: Destiny compass, jewel belt, and ghost map

SPECIAL SKILLS: Over the course of his Quest, Tom has gained many special items for his shield, giving him protection from fire, water, cold, and falling from heights, extra speed in battle, and magic healing ability. He also has the powers he gained from the golden armor, giving him incredible sight, courage, strength, endurance, sword skills, and energy.

⊷ Elenna ⊶

PREFERRED WEAPON: Bow & arrow

ALSO CARRIES: Nothing. Between her bow and her wolf, Silver, Elenna doesn't need anything else!

SPECIAL SKILLS: Not only is Elenna an expert hunter, she is also knowledgeable about boats and water. But most important, she can think quickly in tight spots, which has helped Tom more than once!

⇥ STORM ↤

Tom's horse, a gift
from King Hugo.
Storm's good instincts
and speed have helped
Tom and Elenna from
the very beginning.

⇥ SILVER ↤

Elenna's tame wolf and
constant companion. Not
only is Silver good to have
on their side in a fight,
but the wolf can also help
Tom and Elenna find
food when they're hungry.

⤙ Aduro ⤚

The good wizard of
Avantia and one of Tom's
closest allies. Aduro has
helped Tom many times,
but when Aduro was
captured by Malvel, Tom
was able to repay the
wizard by rescuing him.

⤙ Malvel ⤚

Tom's enemy, determined
to enslave the Beasts of
Avantia and defeat Tom.
This evil wizard rules over
Gorgonia, the Dark
Realm. If he is near,
danger is sure to follow.

All hail, fellow followers of the Quest.

We have not met before but, like you, I have been watching Tom's adventures with a close eye. Do you know who I am? Have you heard of Taladon, the Master of the Beasts? I have returned — just in time for my son, Tom, to save me from a fate worse than death. The evil wizard, Malvel, has stolen something precious from me, and until Tom is able to complete another Quest, I cannot be returned to full life. I must wait between worlds, neither human nor ghost. I am half the man I once was, and only Tom can return me to my former glory.

Will Tom have the strength of heart to help his father? Another Quest can test even the most determined hero. And there may be a heavy price for my son to pay if he defeats six more Beasts. . . .

All I can do is hope — that Tom is successful. Will you put your power behind Tom and wish him well? I know I can count on my son — can I count on you, too? Not a moment can be wasted. As this latest Quest unfolds, much rides on it. We must all be brave.

Taladon

→ PROLOGUE ←

LUKE PEERED CAUTIOUSLY AROUND THE STREET corner. Nothing moved, except for a cat that shot across the cobbles and vanished between two buildings on the opposite side. All the dwellers in Avantia's capital city had gone to their beds long ago.

The moon shed a pale light over the street, though dark shadows lurked in corners. Beyond the rooftops of the shops and houses, Luke could see the purple spires of King Hugo's palace. He shivered as he wondered if Wizard Aduro was looking out, keeping watch on everything that went on in the city.

A hand shoved Luke roughly in the back. He glanced over his shoulder to see his master, Bill.

"What are you waiting for?" Bill demanded. "Get a move on!"

"Just checking," Luke mumbled resentfully.

Luke looked up at the inn's creaking sign above his head: It showed a scarlet dragon with fire spurting from its jaws. Bill pointed to a pile of barrels stacked against the inn wall. "Go on. Climb," he ordered.

Luke hung back. The climb was easy enough: Above the pile of barrels, a drainpipe led up to an open latticed window. But he was scared at the thought of what would happen if anyone found him once he was inside.

"I said *climb*!" Bill gave Luke a harder shove that sent him stumbling to his knees. "You're a young lad — it's easy for you to scramble up there. Get inside, and come down to let me in." He chuckled and rubbed his grimy hands together. "There'll be rich pickings tonight, and you'll get your share."

Luke hauled himself to his feet and limped toward the pile of barrels. He didn't dare disobey Bill. His master was a huge man, tall and broad-shouldered, and he could scare Luke just by glaring at him.

How did I ever end up like this? Luke thought miserably as he started to clamber up the drainpipe. *I never wanted to be a thief.*

As Luke climbed, he thought he could hear soft footfalls in the street, and a sound like a whip cracking in the air. Then he heard the scuffle of Bill's boots on the cobbles, and his master's voice raised in a shout that died away at once in a choking rattle.

Luke peered over his shoulder. Bill was lying facedown in the street. A pool of blood spread slowly from his temple, glistening ink-black in the light of the moon.

Is he dead? Terror froze Luke to the drainpipe.

A moment later Bill stirred, hauling himself to his knees and then to his feet.

"What happened?" Luke called down softly. "Are you all right?"

Bill didn't reply. Staggering forward, he pointed a trembling finger at Luke. "Thief!" he spat, his eyes narrowed. "I'm going to tell your parents what you've been up to!"

Luke gasped in horror. His mother and father would never live down the shame of knowing that he creeped out of bed at night to go thieving with Bill. And Bill might have been rough with him before, but never cruel. What had happened to him?

"You can't —" Luke began.

His protest was cut off by a bloodcurdling howl that echoed through the streets of the city. It sounded like the yowl of a hunting cat, but a thousand times louder and more menacing. Bill cringed at the sound, then turned and raced away.

Luke could see nothing in the empty street except a pair of glittering green dots, dancing in the distance.

"What's that?" he muttered to himself. "They look like eyes."

Cautiously, he began to climb down, only to freeze as the green dots suddenly leaped forward. Out of the night, a coal-black panther appeared, his gleaming fangs bared and his jaws gaping as if he might swallow Luke whole.

With a choking cry, Luke scrambled back up the drainpipe. *Is that what attacked Bill?* he asked himself as he tried to grip the slippery surface.

The panther leaped and snarled beneath him. Swordlike claws slashed at Luke's feet. His teeth were veined like marble, and three tails whipped through the air behind him. Around his neck was a thick leather collar from which dangled an odd-shaped piece of silver.

As Luke watched, a rat scurried out from behind

the pile of barrels. Luke gasped in amazement as the Beast lashed out with one of his tails: He lassoed the squealing rat around the neck and tossed the vermin into his open mouth.

Swallowing the creature in one gulp, the Beast turned back to gaze up at Luke. His emerald eyes burned through the darkness. Luke told his body to move, to keep on clambering up the drainpipe, but he couldn't make his arms and legs obey. His gaze was locked with the Beast's as the panther began to circle one of his three tails. The tail moved faster and faster until it snaked out through the air and snatched Luke's ankle.

Luke kicked out, but he couldn't break the grip of the Beast's tail. His hands scrabbled uselessly at the wall of the inn as he felt himself being dragged down.

He's going to eat me, Luke thought frantically, letting out a shriek of terror. *He'll swallow me up, just like he did that rat. . . .*

CHAPTER ONE

EVIL IN THE CITY

TOM STOOD BESIDE ELENNA ON THE EDGE of the volcano at Stonewin and looked down at the piece of amulet that he held in the palm of his hand. The silver shone in the sunlight and the piece of enamel glowed and winked like a blue eye.

"That's five pieces," he said. "Only one more to go."

Pulling on the leather thong around his neck, he fished the rest of the amulet out from under his tunic and fitted the new piece into place. Silver light flared briefly. When it died away, the new piece had joined with the rest as if it had never been broken off. A jagged gap showed where the final piece was still missing.

"It won't be long now," Elenna said. "Then your father will be fully returned to his old self."

Tom nodded slowly. "But I've lost another of my special powers," he reminded his friend. "I haven't got the strength of heart from the golden chain mail anymore. And that helped me through so many of our Quests."

"You don't need it!" Elenna assured him. "You've got enough courage of your own."

Storm, Tom's black stallion, blew out a noisy breath as if he was agreeing, and Elenna's gray wolf, Silver, gave a long howl.

"See?" Elenna added. "They know you're brave enough for anything! And so does your father."

Tom smiled at her, feeling a wave of determination fill his chest. His father, Taladon, had been captured by the evil wizard, Malvel. Although he had escaped when Tom had completed his third Beast Quest, he was trapped as a ghost between the real world and the spirit world. Taladon could return to life only when the six pieces of the Amulet of Avantia had been joined together again. But Malvel had given the pieces to six Ghost Beasts. Tom had already defeated five of the powerful monsters, but he still had to face the sixth. And he knew that this last Beast would be the deadliest of all.

"So where do we go next?" Elenna asked.

Tom stretched out one hand. "Map!" he commanded.

The ghostly map given to them by Wizard Aduro took shape in front of him, bobbing gently in the air. A shimmering path appeared, leading from the volcano to Avantia's capital city.

"That's where King Hugo's palace is!" Elenna exclaimed. "Surely the Ghost Beast wouldn't dare go there?"

"I don't know." A cold sense of approaching evil creeped through Tom. "Maybe that's what my father meant when he said the next Beast would be 'closer to home.'"

"And more evil than we can possibly know," Elenna added. "He must be really cunning, to hide himself in the very heart of Avantia."

Tom felt his hands ball into fists. "I don't care how cunning he is. We'll defeat him!"

Beside the picture of the city, a small black shape came into view: a panther with a coat the color of night. He snarled and slid out gleaming claws.

At the same moment, a chilly wind blew past Tom, bringing the foul stench of something rotten. The voice of the evil Wizard Malvel whispered in Tom's ear. "Stealth . . ."

"Stealth!" Elenna exclaimed. Clearly she had heard the whisper, too. She exchanged a startled glance with Tom. "Is that the name of the Ghost Beast?"

"It must be," Tom declared. "And we were right. The Beast *is* in the city."

"And that means it's not just our own safety we have to worry about," Elenna said. "The King and everyone else are in danger, too."

Tom's stomach churned with a mixture of fear and excitement. "We'd better get moving," he said. "This Beast could destroy all of Avantia."

Digging into his pocket, Tom drew out the silver compass that his father had given to him. There were two points on it: *Destiny* and *Danger*. He held it out toward the city and watched as the needle swung around to *Destiny*.

"That proves it. There's no time to waste," he said, closing up the compass and stowing it away again. "What's the quickest way of getting to the city?"

"The piece of Tagus's horseshoe will give us extra speed," Elenna said, pointing to the Night Horse's gift, which was fixed onto Tom's shield.

"Yes, but we need to choose the quickest route."

Tom studied the map again, but it showed only

the main road that wound through the hills and fields of Avantia, taking in many towns and villages on its way. He banished the map with a flick of his fingers, and looked around thoughtfully. Then his gaze fell on the mouth of one of the tunnels at the base of the volcano.

"Look!" he cried excitedly, gesturing toward it. "Remember how we rescued the people of Stonewin from the fires of Epos, back on our first Quest?"

"We led them through the tunnels," Elenna replied, her eyes shining as she understood Tom's plan. "They go all the way to the city."

"Yes." A wide grin split Tom's face. "And we can use those tunnels again!"

⇥ CHAPTER TWO ⇤

HELP FROM THE VILLAGE

TOM SET OFF AT A RUN, SPEEDING ALONG THE
path that wound down the side of the volcano. *I
don't need the golden leg armor anymore*, he thought.
Running downhill, I can go as fast as I dare!

Storm cantered ahead, his hooves throwing up
spurts of black volcanic dust, while Elenna and
Silver raced alongside each other, hard on Tom's
heels. Tom loved the feeling of the wind as it
whipped his hair back from his face. *This would be
fun*, he said to himself, *if we weren't on such a serious
Quest.*

Tom slowed his pace to a jog as they reached the
foot of the volcano and headed through the woods.

Now he took the lead, weaving his way through the trees toward the tunnels.

At last Tom and his friends halted, panting, by the mouth of the biggest tunnel. Inside, Tom could see a passageway leading into blackness.

"It's dark," Tom began. "How are we going to —"

He was interrupted by a shout coming from the direction of the village. "Greetings!"

Tom turned to see a group of villagers hurrying toward them. In the lead was Raymond, who had helped guide his people to safety when the volcano was about to erupt. Just behind him was the young boy, Owen, and his mother, Nesta. Owen was still fair-haired and skinny, but much taller than when Tom and Elenna saw him last.

"It's Tom and Elenna!" Raymond exclaimed, throwing his arms around Tom. "What are you doing in these parts?"

"I hope there's no more trouble with Epos," Nesta said as she embraced Elenna.

"No, Epos protects the kingdom now," Tom replied quietly, remembering how the magnificent flame bird had helped him and Elenna in their Quest against Blaze the Ice Dragon. He clapped Owen on the shoulder. "It's good to see you again!"

But even as he spoke, Tom thought that the villagers didn't seem quite as friendly as he remembered them. He had felt a shiver pass through his body as Raymond hugged him. Somehow Owen's mischievous face seemed to have turned cold, and there was a dark glint in Nesta's eyes as she released Elenna. Her sleeves were rolled up, as if she had been working in the kitchen, and there was a long red scratch down one of her arms.

Nesta laughed as she spotted Tom looking at the scratch. "That's nothing!" she assured him, hurriedly rolling her sleeves down. "I got it picking gooseberries. Those thorns!"

"You're welcome to stay with us," Raymond invited them. "We'll never forget what you did for Stonewin."

"Thank you, but we can't stay," Tom replied. He didn't want to share all the details of their Quest, in case word of the Ghost Beasts sent the villagers into a panic. "We have to get back to the city as quickly as we can, so we thought we would go through the tunnels."

"Do you have any candles we could use?" Elenna asked.

"We can do better than that," Raymond told her. "If you come back to the village with us, we'll give you some lamps."

Tom and Elenna exchanged a glance.

"Time's slipping away," Tom muttered into his friend's ear. "We ought to set out as soon as we can."

"We don't seem to have much of a choice," Elenna replied. She pointed to where Owen and the other village children were already clustered around Silver, patting him and running their hands through his thick fur, while one of the adult villagers had taken Storm by the bridle and was leading him away. "Besides, if we don't go to the village, we'll have to *make* torches somehow."

Tom nodded. "And that might take longer than fetching the lamps." He turned to Raymond. "Thanks. We'll come with you, but only to pick up the lamps. It's already late afternoon, and we really need to be on our way."

"Of course!" Raymond smiled as he glanced around at the other villagers. "We'll do everything we can to help."

Another shiver passed through Tom as he saw the jubilant looks some of the villagers were sharing. *Could they be* that *happy we're coming to visit?*

Raymond led the way along a path that wound

through the woods and joined the main street of the village. At the far end was a sturdy hut built of logs. Through the window, Tom could see shelves full of supplies. There were boxes of candles and a row of lamps hanging from the roof.

Raymond flung open the door. "Go in," he said, gesturing to Tom and Elenna. "Take whatever you want."

Tom stepped inside the store, followed by Elenna. He still felt uneasy. He wanted to find what they needed and get out of the village as quickly as they could.

He took several boxes of candles from one of the shelves, shoving the candles into his pockets, while Elenna lifted two of the lamps down from their hooks and carefully filled them with oil from an earthenware jar.

"That should be enough —" Tom began, breaking off at a sharp bang behind him. When he spun around, he saw that the door had slammed shut.

Tom's uneasiness flared into alarm. He ran across to the door and tugged on the handle. But the door wouldn't move.

"It's locked!" Tom exclaimed.

CHAPTER THREE

MALVEL'S PLOT

TOM AND ELENNA RAN TO THE WINDOW, BUT
it was too small to climb through. Outside, the
villagers were crowding around, laughing. Nesta
rolled up her sleeve and waved her scarred arm in
front of Tom and Elenna.

"Gooseberries!" she cried. "Were you really such
fools as to believe that? The three-tailed Beast gave
me this wound, and I'm proud of it!"

"You won't defeat *this* Beast!" Owen added,
rolling up his own sleeve to show a long scratch
from elbow to wrist.

Tom glanced at Elenna. Her eyes were wide

with alarm. "*Three* tails?" she whispered. "What Beast are they talking about?"

Gathering around Nesta, Raymond and the other villagers were showing off their own scratches from the Beast.

"That's what was wrong!" Tom exclaimed, punching at the windowsill in frustration. "I knew there was something. The whole village has been changed!"

One by one, the villagers began to move off, turning their backs and leaving Tom and Elenna in their prison. A man grabbed Storm's bridle and tried to lead him away. The black stallion reared up, his forehooves striking the air as he let out a furious neigh. Silver darted forward, nipping at the man's heels. With a roar of rage, he let go of the bridle. Storm turned and fled down the street in a thunder of hooves, with Silver racing alongside, back toward the tunnels.

"Silver! Silver!" Elenna cried out.

"It's all right." Tom put a hand on her shoulder. "They'll wait for us in the woods. They'd never leave us, but they have more sense than to stay with these evil villagers."

Elenna nodded, though she still looked upset. "At least we don't have to worry about them," she said.

"We need to find out what's going on," Tom decided. "I still have one last power from the golden armor. I can use my magical sight from the golden helmet to look for some clues."

He dragged a wooden box over to the window and scrambled up onto it to give himself the best possible view. *The Beast must have left some traces when he visited the village*, he told himself as he peered down the street. *There might be something to help me track him down.*

He let his magical gaze travel down the street, examining the shops and houses.

"What can you see?" Elenna asked anxiously.

"Nothing yet," Tom replied. "I don't think —
No, wait! What's that?"

He fixed his gaze on a spot beyond the last
houses of the village, where the cobbled street
gave way to a path of beaten earth. In the earth
were huge paw prints leading back toward the
tunnels.

Tom felt the blood drain from his face as he
turned to Elenna. "Paw prints," he murmured
hoarsely. "Huge, like a massive cat's."

Elenna frowned. "I don't understand."

"Don't you see?" Tom jumped down from
the box and stood next to her, pointing out the
window. Inwardly, he cursed himself for not
piecing the evidence together sooner. "The villagers
of Stonewin would never usually behave like this.
Nesta said that a Beast with three tails made the
claw mark on her arm. And all the others have claw
marks, too."

"And there are giant paw prints on the ground!" Elenna exclaimed, suddenly grasping what Tom meant.

"Yes. The Beast that made the marks is the last Ghost Beast. Stealth has attacked the village!"

Elenna nodded slowly. "So that is his evil magic — to turn good people bad!"

Tom looked out the window again, up to the slopes of the volcano. "Do you remember what Malvel said after we defeated Blaze the Ice Dragon? He promised that our next Quest would see evil come home to roost."

"And he really meant it!" Elenna clenched her fists.

"He's kept his promise," Tom agreed. He felt sick with worry for his friends in the city, and for the family he had left behind in Errinel. "Malvel is inflicting the worst thing he possibly could on Avantia. He's trying to turn everyone evil!"

"We've got to get out of here," Elenna said.

"And there's no time to waste." Tom strode back to the door and wrenched the handle again. "Stealth is in the city. What if he has already turned King Hugo and Wizard Aduro evil?"

The lock wouldn't give way to his desperate tugging. Elenna took an arrow out of her quiver and pulled the head off the shaft.

"Maybe I can force the lock," she said as she poked the arrow's point into the keyhole.

Tom watched her for a moment, but she wasn't having any success. The arrowhead was too big to get far enough inside the lock, and the point kept slipping out.

Forcing back panic, Tom began grabbing things from the shelves, tossing aside rolls of linen, jars of nails, and bags of wheat as he searched for something that would help him open the door. Looking at all the useless supplies, his frustration boiled over.

"There's nothing here that will help!"

Elenna straightened up, brushing a lock of hair out of her eyes. "It's no good," she announced.

Tom glanced around frantically. Panic tingled in his belly. He forced himself to take a deep breath. He had to stay calm. *There must be* some *way out of here*, he told himself. *And I'm going to find it!*

CHAPTER FOUR

ESCAPE!

TOM NOTICED A BIG IRON HOOK FIXED TO THE central roof beam of the store. He guessed it was meant for hauling heavy items up onto high shelves. He pictured a rope slung over it, raising a load. . . .

"Yes!" he exclaimed. "That's it!"

He scrabbled among the scattered supplies until he found a coil of thick rope. Unrolling it, he flung one end over the hook, and handed the other to Elenna. "Hold that taut, and brace yourself," he instructed her.

With Elenna gripping the rope, Tom swarmed up it. But as he gazed upward, he spotted the strands fraying where they were looped over the metal hook.

"I'm coming down!" he called to Elenna. "The rope's going to break."

He began climbing rapidly down, but before his feet touched the floor, the rope gave way. With a cry of alarm, Tom plummeted, bruising his shoulder as he hit the ground.

Elenna dropped the rope and knelt beside Tom. "Are you hurt?" she asked anxiously.

Tom sat up, wincing with pain as he massaged his shoulder. "It's nothing much," he said, removing the emerald from his jeweled belt, which he had won from Skor the Winged Stallion.

He pressed it to his shoulder. At once, the pain died away and a cool sensation spread over it. Letting out a sigh of relief, Tom moved his arm up and down to check that the damage was really healed.

"It's fine now," he told Elenna, who was looking on anxiously. "The emerald works really well!"

Tom slotted the token carefully back into his belt and sprang to his feet. He may not be hurt anymore, but they were no nearer to getting out of their prison. "Now what do we do?" he murmured, half to himself. "I'm not trusting that rope again."

"I know!" Elenna exclaimed. She swooped down on one of the rolls of linen Tom had tossed aside while he was searching, and began to tear strips off it. Then she knotted them together to make a rope. As soon as he realized what Elenna was doing, Tom knelt beside her and tested the knots, pulling them as tight as he could.

"It's not perfect," Elenna said, "but it's better than nothing."

"Better than the rope, anyway," Tom agreed.

As soon as the knotted linen was long enough, Tom tossed it over the hook. With Elenna holding the other end, he leaped into the air and swung himself in an arc toward the door. He held his feet braced in front of him, ready for the impact.

As Tom hit the door it started to give way, but the strong wooden planks remained in place.

"Try again!" Elenna cried excitedly.

Tom leaped up and swung himself at the door once more. This time, when his feet slammed into it, the door burst open. Tom smashed through, into the open, scattering splinters of wood everywhere. Triumph surging through him, he landed with a thud, staggered, and regained his balance.

"Come on!" he urged, glancing back at Elenna. "The whole village must have heard that."

Elenna grabbed Tom's shield and thrust it into his hands as she darted out to join him. At the same moment, Tom heard an angry shout from farther down the street. A crowd of men surged out of the inn.

Raymond was in the lead. He spotted Tom and Elenna. "They're escaping!" he shouted.

The whole crowd pounded down the street toward the store hut. Determination surged through Tom. He *wouldn't* let these evil villagers put him and his friend in prison again.

"Let's go!" he yelled.

→ CHAPTER FIVE ←

THROUGH THE TUNNELS

"**WHAT ABOUT THE CANDLES?**" ELENNA GASPED as they began running as fast as they could down the street.

"In my pockets," Tom replied. "Come on!"

The villagers were hard on their heels. Tom cast a rapid glance over his shoulder. Raymond was at the head of the crowd, waving his fists. His flapping shirtsleeves showed the marks of Stealth's claws on his arms.

"Faster!" Tom panted. "They're gaining!"

As he and Elenna turned off the village street and pelted down the path that led to the tunnels, Tom heard the beat of a horse's hooves and the drawn-out howl of a wolf. Storm came cantering out of the trees, with Silver bounding along beside him.

"I knew they wouldn't leave us!" Tom cried out in relief.

As Storm galloped up, Tom grabbed his mane and leaped into the saddle without breaking his stride. Elenna still ran alongside them. Tom reached down to pull her up behind him. They outpaced the villagers as they headed for the tunnels, Silver barking excitedly in the rear.

Outside the largest tunnel entrance, Tom tugged on the reins and brought Storm to a halt. He and Elenna slid to the ground.

"Well done, boy." Tom gave the black stallion a pat on the nose. "You came just in time!"

The sun was going down. The trees cast long shadows and the mouth of the tunnel looked darker than ever. Tom strode up to it. "I hope we're right, and this leads us to the Beast," he said.

"We really need those candles now," Elenna said, peering into the blackness.

Tom pulled a couple of candles out of his pocket. Elenna unfastened the base of her quiver and took out a flint. She struck a flame from it with an arrowhead. The candle flames burned steadily, casting a circle of yellow light as Tom and Elenna stepped into the tunnel.

Tom heard the sound of pounding footsteps outside, and glanced back to see Raymond and the other villagers appearing around a bend in the path.

"Let's go — fast!" he urged Elenna.

With a candle in one hand and Storm's bridle in the other, Tom led the way into the gloomy passage. Elenna followed him, with Silver at her heels. The wolf kept glancing back and letting out threatening howls at the sounds of the pursuing villagers. The noise filled the tunnel with echoes.

The candle flames dipped and wavered as Tom and the others hurried along. They cast moving shadows on the tunnel walls. Storm picked his way among the loose rocks on the tunnel floor, the clatter of his hooves sounding loud in the narrow passage.

Tom paused for a moment to listen. "I can't hear the villagers anymore."

"Good." Elenna patted her wolf friend on the head. "I think Silver must have frightened them off."

Even though they were now safe from the evil villagers, Tom set a brisk pace as they carried on. There was no time to waste as long as Stealth prowled the streets of his beloved kingdom's capital city.

"Which is the right way?" Elenna asked as they came to a place where the passage forked into two.

Tom hesitated, then chose the right-hand tunnel. "I think I remember this from last time," he said.

He led the way up and down rocky slopes, through vast caves, and along passages with roofs so low that Storm could only just fit through. The candles burned down, so Tom and Elenna had to stop and light two more.

Soon afterward, the sound of falling water came from up ahead, and the candle flames lit up a stream that gushed out of the rock above them and fell into a pool below.

"I remember this," Elenna said. She set her candle down on a shelf in the rock so she could cup her hands under the stream and take a drink. "That's good. It's so cold!"

Tom drank, too, and splashed his face, while Storm and Silver lapped from the pool.

As they continued, the tunnel started to slope upward. Tom realized they were drawing close to the caves that opened in the hills just above the city. Excitement fluttered in his stomach. He drew his sword and held it at the ready, alert for any signs that Stealth was nearby.

Eventually, Tom and Elenna climbed up a flight of shallow stone steps.

"We're here!" Elenna exclaimed with a grin of satisfaction.

The steps led into another cave. Tom could see its jagged exit outlined against a starlit sky.

As he stepped onto the hillside, he was about to blow out the candle, when he spotted markings on the ground in front of him. He squatted, holding the flame so its golden light poured down on them. Elenna came to peer over his shoulder.

"Paw prints," Tom whispered, a shiver of horror running through him. "Huge paw prints, just like in the village. Stealth must be waiting for us."

⇥ Chapter Six ⇤

Locked Out

Tom paused outside the city walls. The gates stood open, and beyond them the street was dark and quiet.

"Where are the guards?" Elenna asked, her eyes wide as she gazed around.

"I don't know." Tom felt his heart thumping hard as he led the way through the gates. "And where are all the people?"

Even at this time of day, the city streets were usually full of market stalls, their lamps shining brightly on fruit and cheese or freshly baked bread and biscuits. The citizens would shop and gossip, while children darted to and fro among the stalls.

But there were no lights, no sounds of voices or laughter. All the doors and windows were tightly shut.

Storm's hooves sounded loud on the cobbles as Tom led him through the streets. Silver padded close to Elenna's side, his muzzle raised to sniff the air. The hairs on his neck were bristling as if he could sense an enemy, though there was nothing to be seen.

"It's like a ghost town," Elenna whispered.

"Or a town ruled by a Ghost Beast," Tom added grimly.

As they turned a corner, Tom caught a glimpse of two flashes of emerald green. Silver growled deep in his throat. Tom grabbed the hilt of his sword, but as he drew it, the two emerald flashes darted away into the night.

Tom shivered. "I think we just spotted Stealth."

Elenna nodded, looking around apprehensively. "Where did he go?"

"I don't know. But we had better keep our eyes open."

As Tom finished speaking, a threatening snarl curled through the air from behind. Tom whipped around. How could the Beast have gotten there so quickly? He glanced rapidly around them, his sword at the ready, but nothing moved in the darkness.

"This Beast is very good at *hiding*," Elenna remarked.

Tom nodded. "Stealth is no coward," he said. "He'll show himself when he's ready."

The thought of a Ghost Beast stalking them made every hair on Tom's head prickle with tension, but he strode on determinedly toward the palace. "We've got to make sure King Hugo and Wizard Aduro are safe," he said.

At last, the street they were following led into the square in front of the palace. The gates to the palace grounds stood open, just like the gates to the city.

"There are no guards here, either," Elenna murmured.

They could see no lights on in the palace as they passed through the gates, but as they approached the building, lamplight suddenly flickered through a window just above the main door. Tom looked up to see King Hugo gazing out. His face looked ghostly pale.

"Greetings, sire!" Tom called out, relieved that the King was still alive.

King Hugo did not reply. He stared down at Tom and Elenna as if he was afraid of them.

Feeling even more uneasy, Tom tried to push open the palace door, but it didn't budge. He rattled the handle, but the door still didn't move. It was locked!

"Please let us in, sire," he called up to the King. "We've brought news."

For a moment, King Hugo didn't reply. Tom exchanged a mystified glance with Elenna. He didn't understand this. He had never been denied entry to the palace before.

Another figure moved up beside King Hugo to look out the window.

"Father!" Tom cried out as he recognized Taladon.

Taladon didn't speak, either. After a moment, he shook his head sadly and moved away from the window again.

"Father, what's the matter?" Tom called. He felt as if the ground had just opened up beneath his feet. For his father to turn away from him like that, something must be really wrong. Tom thought he would burst with frustration if he didn't find out what it was.

Taladon didn't reappear, but King Hugo pushed the window open and leaned out. "I'm sorry, Tom," he said. "We can't let you in. Stealth has been rampaging through the city. Every time he scratches someone, they turn to evil. No one can be trusted." The King hesitated, his face filled with grief. "I'm not even sure I can trust you and Elenna," he went on at last. "Pull up your sleeves, and let me see if you carry any panther claw marks."

As Tom hesitated, he felt Elenna's hand on his arm. "King Hugo is right," she whispered. "We trusted the people of Stonewin, and remember how easily they tricked us! The King is doing the only thing he can — protecting the last sanctuary in Avantia. If the evil Beast got into the palace, then everything would be lost."

Tom let out a long breath. Elenna was right. If Avantia came to be ruled by an evil king, there would be no hope left. But it still hurt him to see mistrust in the eyes of the King he loved and served.

There was no point in pulling up his sleeves; he and Elenna could be carrying the marks of Stealth anywhere on their bodies.

"I understand, sire," Tom replied. "Just tell me one thing — is Wizard Aduro safe?" His stomach lurched to think of Stealth scratching the good wizard and turning him into another Malvel.

King Hugo nodded. "He is safe," he replied. "But his magic cannot undo the work of the Beast."

Tom bowed to the King and turned away. He paced through the gates again, followed by Elenna and their animal friends, and halted as another ghostly snarl swept across the empty square. Somewhere out there, a Beast was stalking the streets of the city. And Tom knew that it was his job to defeat him.

"While there's blood in my veins," he vowed, "I'll save Avantia!"

CHAPTER SEVEN

THE CLAWS OF STEALTH

TOM AND ELENNA CREEPED THROUGH SHIFTING light and darkness as clouds scudded across the face of the moon. The city streets were empty, but Tom knew that every corner, doorway, or abandoned market stall could conceal Stealth.

He lugged aside a barrel full of trash to peer into the corner behind it, but he only disturbed a rat, which scuttled quickly away. On the other side of the street, Elenna was peering down a stairwell into the doorway of someone's basement.

"Nothing here!" she called softly to Tom.

His sword at the ready, Tom led them farther away from the palace. All the while, he was alert for the flash of emerald eyes or the sound of evil snarling. But there was no sign of the Ghost Beast.

Suddenly, Tom heard the sound of a door crashing open. Loud voices echoed in the still air, and the thud of footsteps came rapidly closer.

Elenna tugged at Tom's arm. "Quick — hide!"

Tom led Storm into the mouth of a narrow alley. Elenna and Silver followed and pressed themselves against the wall. Peering out of the shadows, Tom saw a group of men and women burst into the street from around the nearest corner.

Their clothes were filthy and ragged. Tom could make out Stealth's claw marks on some of them. All of them held weapons — knives, hammers, and mallets. Their eyes seemed to glow with rage as they stumbled past the mouth of the alley. They banged on closed doors or pulled up cobbles from the street to throw at shuttered windows. Tom caught a glimpse of a man peering out from one of the houses, wide-eyed with terror, before slamming the shutters closed.

Tom felt sick as he watched them go. The citizens had been happy until the claws of Stealth had changed them. He tightened his grip on his sword, more determined than ever to find the ghostly panther and defeat him.

Elenna put a hand comfortingly on Tom's arm. "Maybe they'll be all right again," she suggested. "Just as soon as Stealth is dead."

They emerged from the alley and went on with their search, but the city was silent again and Stealth had not reappeared.

"This is hopeless," Tom said at last, halting beside a large inn on a street corner. "It will be dawn soon, and what will we do then? It could be dangerous to stay in the city in daylight."

"You mean it's not dangerous now?" Elenna's mouth twisted in a wry grin. "What's the matter with Silver?" she added. The wolf had raised his muzzle and was sniffing the air, his hackles rising. "Can you smell something, boy?"

Suddenly alert, Tom spun around. At the same instant, a loud yowling split the silence. A huge black shape launched itself from the roof of the inn. Silver's warning had given Tom the seconds he needed to leap out of the way.

Stealth landed on the cobbles, panting lightly as the gaze from his emerald-green eyes locked with Tom's. His gleaming white fangs were bared in a snarl.

Tom heard an answering snarl coming from Silver's throat. The wolf's fur was bristling, his muscles tensed to leap at the fierce panther. Stealth towered over them, claws unsheathed, ready to strike.

"Elenna, keep back," Tom warned. "Don't let Silver or Storm come near." He thought with horror, *What would happen if* we *were turned to evil?*

"Silver!" Elenna's voice was commanding. "Silver, come here. You can't help."

The gray wolf let out a whine of protest, but he obeyed Elenna and followed her.

Tom was aware of his friend leading Storm and Silver farther down the alley beside the inn, but he kept his gaze fixed on the Ghost Beast. He had never seen anything like it before.

Stealth's green eyes sparkled like gems. His claws glittered. His huge ears swiveled back and forth, twitching at the slightest noise. But what turned the blood in Tom's veins to ice was the Beast's three tails, slashing through the air like whips.

Around the panther's neck was a thick leather collar, from which hung a scrap of silver. Tom's heart beat faster as he spotted it. The last piece of the Amulet of Avantia! If only he could get the fragment, his Quest would be complete. His father would no longer be a ghost.

Tom knew he couldn't risk coming within range of Stealth's claws or his three lashing tails. Raising his sword, he sent it whirling through the air in a shining arc. Stealth crouched to leap at Tom, but before he could take off, the spinning sword sliced through one of his tails, and fell clattering to the cobbles.

Blood as black as night spurted from the wound, and Stealth let out a howl of rage and pain. Tom's eyes widened as the Beast shifted into his ghostly form: His body changed into churning black smoke, outlined by shimmering scarlet light.

No! Tom thought. *Stealth is changing into his ghostly form to hide himself from me. How can I defeat a Beast I can't see?*

Tom darted forward to retrieve his sword. Immediately, the panther changed back into flesh and blood, giving a terrifying snarl.

"You don't scare me, Stealth!" Tom called out bravely.

Stealth crouched on the cobbles, ready to spring at him. Tom was caught between the Beast and the wall of the inn. His sword lay out of reach, almost underneath the paws of the Beast.

An arrow whipped through the air from behind him, striking the panther between his green eyes. Stealth tossed his head with a snarl of fury, giving Tom the chance to grab his sword and scramble back, out of range.

"Thanks, Elenna!" he shouted as another arrow struck the Beast in the shoulder.

Stealth bared his teeth menacingly. Tom could see how hungry he was for revenge. The huge Beast leaped into the air, his vast black shadow enveloping Tom. At the last second, Tom jumped aside.

But he didn't have his magical leaping power anymore. As his feet hit the uneven cobbles, he stumbled and fell awkwardly onto his side, knocking the breath out of his body.

Must move away, Tom thought, half-stunned. *Must get up . . .*

But his body wouldn't obey him. Unable to move, he watched with horror as Stealth stretched out one paw, his deadly claws bared, ready to attack.

Chapter Eight

Elenna to the Rescue

"**No!**" Elenna yelled.

Before the Beast's claws could scratch down Tom's arm, he saw his friend pull another arrow from her quiver. "Don't get too close!" he gasped.

Elenna loosed the arrow. It struck Stealth on the back of the neck and stuck there, quivering. The Ghost Beast snarled and twisted his head, his jaws snapping as he tried to grasp the arrow and pull it out.

Elenna ran forward and grabbed Tom by the arm, hauling him to his feet and back out of range.

"Thanks!" Tom panted.

Shivers ran through Tom's body as he realized what would have happened if his friend hadn't been so quick. He would have been turned to evil. . . . Avantia's last hope would have been gone.

"We need a different plan," he said to Elenna. "I can't risk getting near those claws."

Elenna nodded, but didn't reply. She was still watching the furious Beast, her bow raised and another arrow notched on the string.

Tom remembered how he had swung himself through the air to escape from the store back in Stonewin. *That's it!* he told himself. *I need a rope!* If he could lasso Stealth and climb onto his back, the Ghost Beast wouldn't be able to reach him with his claws. *And then I can rescue the piece of the amulet from his collar*, Tom thought.

Glancing around, he saw a pile of barrels stacked up beside the wall of the inn, bound together by a piece of rope. Tom sheathed his sword and darted over to them, tugging desperately at the knotted coils.

Behind him, Tom heard a delighted snarl, and glanced over his shoulder to see that Stealth had finally wrenched the arrow out of his flesh. His gleaming teeth splintered the shaft and he tossed the scraps away.

I've got to get this rope loose now! Tom thought.

Stealth crouched again, snarling as he prepared to leap at Tom. At the same instant, the knot gave way and Tom pulled the rope free from the barrels.

Tom quickly twisted the rope to form a noose. As Stealth pounced, Tom ducked, and the huge panther leaped over him, whipping around as he landed to face Tom again.

Tom tossed the noose into the air and began to circle the panther. The Ghost Beast lashed out at him, but he was too big to maneuver himself properly in the narrow alley.

"Move back," Tom instructed Elenna. "We need more space. If we have to fight, we'll fight fair."

With his gaze fixed on the panther, he heard Elenna leading Storm away and the patter of Silver's paws on the cobbles. Tom followed them, walking backward, circling the lasso over his head. Stealth stalked along the alley after him, his tails raking along the walls on either side.

As he emerged from the end of the alley, Tom realized that in their search for Stealth, he and Elenna had traced a circle through the city. They had arrived back in the main square, not far from the palace gates. Glancing up at the palace, Tom spotted the one lighted window, with King Hugo, Wizard Aduro, and his father, Taladon, all watching silently. *They've never seen anything like this*, Tom thought. *I only hope I come out the winner.*

Stealth had emerged from the alley, too, and was patiently prowling across the square toward Tom.

Circling the lasso, Tom tried to judge the best moment to strike.

"Tom, be careful!" Elenna's voice had a warning note.

He realized that Stealth understood what he was trying to do. The Beast was circling one of his tails above his head, making a lasso of his own.

If he catches me, I'm done for, Tom told himself. *It's now or never!* He had to lasso the Beast before the Beast lassoed him first. And he could see that Stealth's body was gradually beginning to fade into its ghostly form.

I've got to catch him before he changes!

Tom sent the rope arcing through the air toward the panther. At the same time, Elenna fired a volley of arrows at the Beast's back legs. Stealth's head snapped around and he bared his teeth at her. The Beast had turned half-ghostly, but Tom could just make out enough of him to aim.

"Yes!" Tom's triumphant shout echoed across the square as the noose fell perfectly over the Ghost Beast's head.

Tom pulled the rope tight around Stealth's neck and ran to his side. Distracted by the struggle, it was clear that Stealth could no longer concentrate on becoming a ghost, and he returned to his full form. Gripping the panther's collar in one hand, Tom vaulted onto the Beast's back. Stealth struggled to wrench the rope out of Tom's hands, but Tom held it fast.

Stealth swung his head around, his fangs snapping at Tom, but every time he turned to get closer, Tom was carried out of reach on the Beast's own body. The rope burned his hands as he clung to it, trying to stay on the ghost panther's twisting back.

Sitting astride the Beast, Tom drew his sword again, gripping the rope with his other hand. He managed to scramble to his feet, but almost lost his balance as Stealth reared up on his hind legs, in an effort to shake Tom off. The panther's coal-black fur was as slippery as ice under Tom's feet. But he somehow clung to the rope and climbed up Stealth's spine until he was in reach of the collar.

With a single stroke, Tom sliced the collar through. It clattered to the ground, the piece of amulet ringing on the cobblestones of the square.

Stealth let out a final roar of pain and anger.

At the same instant, a fierce gust of wind blew through the square. A whirling reddish-purple cloud began to form in front of Tom, and a scream of rage echoed through the air. "Nooooooo!"

Tom recognized the voice. *That's Malvel!*

⇥ CHAPTER NINE ⇤

FIGHT AGAINST THE WIZARD

Tom scrambled down Stealth's leg to ground level. Stealth growled and began tugging at the rope to free himself. The reddish-purple cloud thickened, and evil Wizard Malvel stepped out of it. His sunken eyes burned with rage. As his dark cloak flapped like the wings of a hawk, he swooped to grab the collar and the last piece of the amulet.

But Tom was too quick for him. He stepped forward, kicking the collar out of the wizard's reach, and held his sword at Malvel's throat. The evil wizard staggered back, rage and fear in his eyes.

As Tom tried to follow him, Stealth slipped between them. His body was starting to turn ghostly again, though Tom could still see his faint outline.

Tom tried to dart between Stealth's ghostly legs to reach Malvel, but the panther moved to block him. Tom's outstretched arm passed through the Beast's smoky body. The icy touch made his arm numb, and he stumbled back, barely able to keep hold of his sword.

Recovering quickly, Tom made another dash for Malvel, but once again Stealth got in his way. *This Beast is too clever!* Tom thought angrily.

Malvel raised his hands, ready to cast a spell. As he began to chant in a thunderous voice, Tom shivered and thought, *I've no protection against magic!*

Tom braced himself for a desperate leap at the evil wizard. But then he heard Elenna's voice. "Tom! Here — catch!"

His friend had grabbed Stealth's collar from the ground. She tossed it to Tom, who caught it in his free hand. Triumph flooded through him. *Now I've got all the pieces of the Amulet of Avantia!*

As soon as Tom's fingers closed around the collar, dazzling light poured out of the scrap of silver, forming a protective orb around him. Purple fire streamed from Malvel's fingers, but when it hit the orb, it ricocheted off harmlessly and disappeared.

Malvel let out a shriek of rage as his spell failed. Tom lunged forward. "Avantia!" he cried, slicing his sword through the air. Malvel leaped away, but the tip of Tom's sword scored through his flesh, opening a gash in his cheek.

The evil wizard screamed again with pain and fury. "You'll regret that, boy!"

Before Tom could strike him again, he stepped back into the cloud, which exploded in a burst of

purple light. Tom had to shield his eyes against it. The silver orb that had protected him died away, too.

Stealth's ghostly form whipped around to attack. Gripping his sword, Tom braced himself for the strike. But the smoky shape with its faint outline of crimson fire began to fade. Tom heard the last echo of a snarl as the Beast vanished completely.

Tom stood panting, gazing at the spot where the Ghost Beast had disappeared. "He's gone," he said in a hoarse voice. "Stealth is gone for good."

Elenna hurried to his side, with Storm and Silver close behind her. "Tom, that was great!"

"I wouldn't have survived if you hadn't thrown me the piece of amulet," Tom replied. "And I only managed to wound Malvel. That slash on his cheek won't kill him."

"You're right, boy." Malvel's voice spoke from the emptiness. He spat a curse at Tom. "Our fight is far from over. I'll be back!"

"Good!" Tom called out in reply. "I look forward to it." Remembering the look of fury and frustration on the dark wizard's face as blood poured from his cheek, Tom felt courage surge through him. If Malvel could be wounded, he could be killed! If he ever had to face the evil wizard again, Tom had some extra knowledge about him now. But he could think about that another day. Turning to Elenna, he added, "We've finished our Quest! And now I can meet my father properly."

➤ CHAPTER TEN ↢

HOME TO ERRINEL?

SHOUTING BROKE OUT BEHIND TOM. HE SPUN around, his sword at the ready, braced for another attack.

The citizens of Avantia were flinging open the doors and windows of the houses around the square. They streamed out into the streets, laughing and shouting joyfully as they surrounded Tom and Elenna.

"We're free!"

"Well done! You killed the Beast!"

Tom sheathed his sword, almost overwhelmed by all the people who wanted to shake his hand or clap him on the shoulder. He pushed the collar,

• 71 •

with the last precious piece of the amulet, into his pocket in case he might drop it in the crowd.

"I did what I had to do," he said. "And I couldn't have done it without Elenna."

Elenna grinned at his praise.

Then the people grew quiet, and moved back. Tom saw that the palace door had opened, and King Hugo was striding across the square toward him. Tom began to kneel as his King approached, but King Hugo grasped him by the shoulders and drew him into an embrace.

"You've saved Avantia!" he exclaimed. Releasing Tom, he added, "I'm sorry for locking you out of the palace. The risk was just too great."

"I understand," Tom replied. "You were only trying to protect Avantia."

With an arm around his shoulders, King Hugo led Tom back toward the palace. Elenna followed, leading Storm, with Silver bounding alongside.

A golden light was growing beyond the palace roof, showing where the sun would rise. Malvel's evil had vanished along with the night.

Inside the palace courtyard, a servant led Storm away to be groomed and fed, while King Hugo took Tom and Elenna inside. Silver padded quietly along behind.

The King led Tom and Elenna down the stairs and along a stone passage to a heavy door studded with brass nails.

"This is the armor room," Tom said.

"That's right," said King Hugo. "And the very end of your Quest will happen here."

Tom followed him into the room. It was familiar to him from the start of his second Beast Quest, when he recovered the golden armor. He remembered the rough stone walls and the torches in metal holders, and the wooden stand for the armor that stood in the middle of the room.

King Hugo's master of arms stood beside the wooden stand. He smiled as he saw Tom and Elenna. "Welcome back," he said. His pet ferret poked its head out of his pocket and added a friendly squeak.

Silver let out a questioning whine as he spotted the little creature, and Elenna rested a hand on his neck. "It's all right, boy," she murmured. "He's a friend."

Wizard Aduro stepped forward. "Well done, Tom," he said. "Your courage has saved Avantia once again."

Embarrassed, Tom exchanged a glance with Elenna. "We did it together."

"And now you must finish your Quest," Aduro went on. "Come."

He gestured for Tom to approach a small table that stood beside the wall. A crimson velvet cushion lay upon it. "This is the rightful resting place of the Amulet of Avantia," he said.

Tom took the leather thong from around his neck and laid the amulet carefully on the velvet cushion. Then he pulled Stealth's collar out of his pocket and unfastened the final scrap of silver. He fitted it carefully into the gap that waited for it.

Silver light flared up, filling the room and dazzling Tom's eyes. He heard Elenna gasp in surprise.

When the light faded, Tom saw that the Amulet of Avantia was complete once again. He drew a long breath of satisfaction. *That's what King Hugo meant. Now my Beast Quest is really over.*

"Tom, look!" Elenna exclaimed.

Tom turned to see that the suit of golden armor had reappeared on the wooden stand. The master of arms had already taken out a handkerchief and was polishing the gleaming breastplate.

Then a man stepped out from behind the golden armor. Tom caught his breath as he recognized his father. But he had never seen Taladon looking like this. He seemed taller and broader than ever. His eyes shone and the pink of good health glowed in his cheeks.

He put his arms around Tom in a tight embrace. This time Tom could feel his warmth and strength. It was how he had always dreamed of meeting his father.

"Congratulations, Tom," Taladon said, stepping back. "And you, too, Elenna. I'm proud of you both. I knew you wouldn't fail."

"The whole of Avantia owes them thanks," Wizard Aduro said.

King Hugo led the way out of the armor room and back up the stairs into his throne room. The balcony windows stood open, and Tom could hear the sound of the crowd outside in the square.

"Come, Taladon," King Hugo said. "I must announce your return."

The noise outside swelled to a welcoming roar as King Hugo and Taladon stepped out onto the balcony. Tom and Elenna followed them out with Silver close beside Elenna.

Morning sunlight lit up the square and the crowds of people, who were still streaming in from all directions. King Hugo raised his hands for silence, but it was a while before he could make himself heard.

"Good citizens of Avantia," he began, "I bring you wonderful news. Taladon the Swift has returned to the kingdom!"

Taladon stepped forward to take a bow and the crowd went wild, waving and cheering and tossing their hats into the air.

"Now that Taladon is here, what are you going to do?" Elenna asked Tom, as his father waved to the crowd.

Tom heard a footstep behind him and looked around to see that Wizard Aduro was watching them closely, a gentle smile on his face. "Are you glad your journey is over?" he asked. "Do you want to go home to Errinel?"

Tom opened his mouth to reply, and stopped. He had often felt homesick for his village and longed to see his aunt and uncle again, but he found it hard to imagine settling back into life at the forge.

Something in Aduro's voice, or the gleam in his eyes, sent a prickle of knowledge creeping up Tom's spine. "I'm not going back to Errinel, am I?"

Aduro shook his head. As the cheers of the crowd echoed in their ears, he drew Tom and Elenna back into the shadows of the throne room.

"You will have some time to spend with your father," the good wizard promised. "But after that, you may be needed elsewhere." His finger curled, beckoning. "Follow me. I have something to show you. . . . The most difficult Quests are yet ahead."

Tom exchanged a glance with Elenna. He didn't know what Wizard Aduro meant, but he realized that his path was leading him to new dangers. His breath came faster, and he shivered with a mixture of fear and excitement.

Am I ready? he asked himself.

Beside him, Elenna's eyes were shining, and Silver had cocked his head alertly, as if he wanted to set out right away.

Yes! Tom straightened his shoulders as triumph flooded through him. *While there's blood in my veins, I'll serve Avantia!*

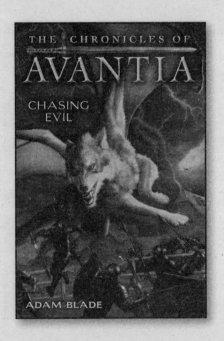